Puppies! Puppies! Puppies! Puppies!

Susan Meyers

Illustrated by David Walker

SCHOLASTIC INC.

New York Toronto London Auckland Sydney
Mexico City New Delhi Hong Kong Buenos Aires

Artist's Note

I start every painting with a pencil sketch. When I've done a drawing I like, I place it on a light table and tape heavy paper on top of it. I then begin layering color after color until the painting looks finished. The first color I paint on the paper is usually brown; the last things I paint are characters' eyes. I use acrylic paint and several different sizes of artist's brushes.

Designed by Becky Terhune

ISBN 0-439-85548-9

Published by Scholastic Inc.
SCHOLASTIC and associated logos are trademarks and/or registered trademarks of Scholastic Inc.

12 11 10 9 8 7 6 5 4 3 2 1   6 7 8 9 10 11/0

Printed in the U.S.A.   08
This edition first printing, January 2006

To Cody and his many moms—Ruth, Anna,
Nancy, Diana, and, of course, Candy
—S.M.

For my wonderful Olivia, the best
friend a puppy could ever have
—D.W.

Puppies big and puppies small,
Puppies short and puppies tall.

Spotty, wrinkly, shaggy puppies,
Bouncy, wriggly, waggy puppies.

Here and there and everywhere,
Puppies! Puppies! Puppies!

Puppies born with eyes shut tight,
In the middle of the night.

Nursing in a snuggly row,
Drinking milk to make them grow.

Getting bigger every day,
Eyes wide open. Time to play!

Tumbling, wrestling, racing puppies,
Tugging, chewing, chasing puppies.

Here and there and everywhere,

Puppies! Puppies! Puppies!

Puppies going to new homes,
With a family all their own.

Getting bowls and beds and names,

Finding toys, inventing games.

Meeting people old and young,
Making friends with everyone.

Cuddling, kissing,
napping puppies,
Yowling, howling,
yapping puppies.

Here and there and everywhere,

Puppies! Puppies! Puppies!

Puppies chewing shoes and slippers,
Rugs and mops and swimming flippers.

Leaving puddles on the floor,
Sneaking out the kitchen door.

Digging holes and making noise,

Running off with baby's toys.

Shredding, tearing, breaking puppies,

Messy, trouble-making puppies.

Here and there and everywhere,

Puppies! Puppies! Puppies!

Puppies going off to school,
Collars, leashes, that's the rule.

Learning how to sit and stay,
Getting treats when they obey.

Washed and brushed and clipped and combed,
Winning ribbons when they're shown.

Fine and fancy-dancy puppies,
Clever, smart, and prancy puppies.

Here and there and everywhere,

Puppies! Puppies! Puppies!

Puppies who just grew and grew,

Into dogs with things to do.

Leading people on the go,

Pulling sleds through ice and snow.

Chasing squirrels,
herding sheep,
Guarding children
while they sleep.

Working, playing, being friends,
Perhaps becoming parents, then . . .

Here and there and everywhere,

Puppies!
Puppies!
Puppies!